Cassian

A Vampire's Mate Novella

Grae Bryan

Contents

One

Cass

O *h, so it's like a* grown-up *bar*, was all Cass could think as he entered the
hushed space, all soft lighting and dark wood; small, intimate tables; and
leather-backed chairs. It was nothing like the boisterous sports bars or clubs he'd
ventured into since turning twenty-one, the best that his little college town had
to offer, all places aimed at university kids who wanted to get wild, loud, laid, or
all of the above.

This was the kind of place where people ordered wine, or cocktails, or if beer,
definitely the kind that came in, like, some sort of frosted glass. But that was okay.
That was fine, really. Because yes, Cass may have technically been a college kid,
and yes, he was most definitely interested in maybe, possibly (hopefully) getting
laid, but he was also an adult, with just as much right to be there as anyone else,
okay?

Cass found an empty spot at the bar and hopped onto the stool, silently cursing
the fact that it was tall enough for his stupidly short legs to dangle.

The bartender was in front of him in an instant. "Need a menu?"

Cass shook his head, not wanting to get overwhelmed by choices when he'd
barely been brave enough to walk through the doors in the first place. "Um, just
a manhattan?"

He hated that it came out as a question.

"Right after I see some ID." The man gave him a kind smile as he said it, but
he definitely wasn't joking.

Cass couldn't exactly blame him—he'd always looked younger than his age, and his outfit choice of fussy button-up and pressed pants had somehow only enhanced the effect. So he fished his ID out of his wallet and handed it over.

The bartender looked it over thoughtfully. "Barely legal, huh?"

Cass couldn't help it: he fucking blushed. Not exactly the secret to looking like he belonged, he was pretty sure. It was just, the guy made it sound all dirty or something.

The bartender cocked a brow at his flushed cheeks but was kind enough not to comment. He just shot Cass a wink. "Coming right up, then, cutie."

Oh. *Oh.* That was flirting, right? Was Cass allowed to flirt back, or would that be frowned upon? Could he get the bartender to take him home, maybe? That would be pretty cool, right?

But even as he was thinking it, he was glancing at his phone for the fifteenth time that night, seeing if he had a text from Blake. Pathetic.

There was nothing since the last: *Going to grab a beer with some new ski buddies. You up for it?*

Cass had never responded. Because he knew—he absolutely *knew*—what it was going to be like. Some gorgeous, tanned, athletic ski bunnies draped over Blake's massive shoulders, licking their lips like he was some kind of human candy. And why shouldn't they? Blake was gorgeous. Blake was perfect. Blake was...

Blake was everything.

Cass had been stunned when they'd been roomed together for their junior year. He knew at this point most people chose their own roommates, and he knew why *he* hadn't done so: college hadn't exactly been the social awakening he'd hoped for. Which was his own fault, choosing a known party school just because he'd had a full scholarship. But Blake? Cass had sized him up in an instant: handsome, popular, able to make friends like it was as simple as breathing. The fact that he'd chosen a random assignment had made zero sense in Cass's eyes. But Blake had said something about getting his grades up and not needing the distraction of his rowdy friends. And so Cass—uncool, untalented, loner Cass—had suddenly been paired up with one of the university's golden gods.

Blake was everything Cass wasn't. Blake played intramural sports, was built like a linebacker, and collected girls' numbers like they were spare change. Not that Cass wanted any girls' numbers. He'd take some guys' numbers, for sure. He'd take Blake's number, was the stupid, horrible, evil truth of it.

Well, he had Blake's number. Obviously. They were roommates, after all. But he didn't have it *that* way. He had it, like, *Hey dude, got any spare quarters for the laundromat?* Or, *Grabbing food, want me to bring some back?*

Because that was the other thing. The other, completely unfair thing that had become clear over time. Blake was nice. Like, super nice. He'd never made Cass feel inferior or small (except maybe just by existing), despite their many differences. He treated Cass like he was special, like he was smart and funny and not at all a complete drag to be around.

Which didn't help Cass's stupid crush one bit. What also didn't help was his suggestion they road-trip home for spring break together. They were apparently both from Phoenix, despite never having crossed paths before college. And then had come his suggestion they stop in some place called Hyde Park so Blake could hit the slopes for the weekend, taking advantage of the last few snowy mountain days before warmer weather took over.

And now they were here, and Cass was as hopeless as ever. He'd spent the day exploring the town instead of the mountain, because a day spent falling on his butt on the packed snow did *not* sound like the funnest of fun times to him personally. And he'd hoped they'd maybe at least get dinner after, and Cass could have tried not to gawk as Blake was his usual charming, sweet self over burgers and beers. But of course Blake had made friends on the slopes, and of course he was going to hang out with whatever fun, popular, athletic crowd he'd found. Which left Cass—

"So deep in thought."

Cass startled, accidentally flicking the coaster he'd been toying with up and over the beer. Oops. He hadn't even quite realized his drink was in front of him, drops of condensation already forming on the glass. And apparently the stool next to him was no longer empty but occupied by some handsome, older dude.

Not *Blake* handsome, of course, but kind of...compelling? And he was talking to *Cass*.

Cass tried to pull his brain out of its Blake spiral and respond like an adult, casting a sidelong glance at the stranger. "Oh yeah. You know."

Jesus. Was that the best he could do?

The man's lips curled ever so slightly. "I'm afraid I don't. Pretty thing like you, what need do you have to be scowling so?"

Pretty. Pretty? No, that wasn't right. Cass was... He was just boring. Dirty-blond hair he could never get to sit flat. Washed-out blue eyes. Skinny and short and often at odds with his own limbs.

But this guy was looking at him like he was—like he was some sort of snack. And Cass was sitting there, stupidly saying nothing. He tried to come out with something passable. "Just roommate stuff."

"Ah." The man sipped his cocktail. "An irritant?"

"No!"

Cass's denial came out more strongly than he intended, but the man just gave him that same subdued smile. "Sloppy, perhaps?"

Cass shook his head. "Nuh-uh."

"Loud banging headboards till the wee hours?"

Cass coughed as he tried to sip his manhattan. That one wasn't exactly inaccurate. "A crush," he admitted sheepishly, once he got his windpipe back under control. Because fuck it, they were only in this town for two nights—he was never gonna see this guy again. Who cared if he knew Cass was head over heels for an unattainable roommate, one he would never meet?

Another, "Ah," this one full of understanding. "Yes." The man nodded. "I vaguely recall such things."

"You can't be that old," Cass teased. The guy was probably late thirties at most. But maybe people grew out of their hopeless crushes when they left their twenties. Wouldn't that be great?

"Older than you might think." The man's eyes flashed in amusement, and then he was waving the bartender over for another round. "Well, we'll just have to distract you from your thoughts, won't we?"

And distract he did. He was actually pretty good at it, asking Cass question after question without revealing anything about himself. He also kept buying the drinks, which was generous of him, especially when Cass started turning into an embarrassingly maudlin drunk. "Just wish I was special, ya know? But 'm boring. Boooooring. And a guy."

"What's wrong with your gender?"

"Blake likes girls."

"Ah. I see." The man—Cass was pretty sure he'd given a name at some point, maybe Anton? Or Arthur?—leaned closer. He was honestly pretty close already, having scooted his barstool nearer to Cass at some point during their tipsy discussion. He had a strange scent about him up close, almost like old pennies. "What if you *could* be special, Cass? What if you could be...quite unique."

Cass smiled dopily, his head feeling heavy from the numerous manhattans. "That'd be cool."

And then Maybe-Arthur was holding his hand, tugging lightly. "Come with me."

Cass was just tipsy enough to say yes. This was the whole reason he'd come out: to try to find someone else to hook up with, to try to get over his stupid crush, to try to finally shed his ever-stubborn virginity, even. So what if this guy wasn't Blake? So what if Blake was never, ever going to want him? *This* guy maybe wanted him. And it would be nice to be kissed, to be touched. And he'd said he thought Cass was pretty. He looked at him like he was not just a snack but a whole meal.

They shuffled—or Cass shuffled, his companion seemingly able to walk just fine—and Cass was vaguely surprised when, instead of to a cab, the guy directed him to the alley outside the bar. Maybe-Arthur leaned in, that old-penny scent lingering again. Was he going to kiss Cass? His eyes were the wrong color, brown instead of green. But who cared, right? Blake was probably doing the same with some ski harlot.

But the guy leaned into Cass's ear instead. "Now, I don't like my dinner quite so soaked in alcohol," he whispered. "But you really are an adorable creature. I think I'll make an exception."

And then he was kissing Cass's neck, which was sort of okay. But the soft kiss didn't last long, quickly followed by a sudden, sharp sting. And then Cass was gasping through a weird flood of arousal, something that had been missing this whole interaction because the guy wasn't *Blake*.

And Maybe-Arthur wasn't taking his mouth off Cass's neck. If anything, he was latched on. And he was...swallowing?

He's drinking me, Cass thought, wondering if he was going insane. *He's drinking my blood.*

By the time Cass fought through the haze of alcohol and surprise enough to think to struggle, his limbs were too heavy to lift.

Oh God. He was dying, right? This was what dying felt like.

His eyes fell closed, and he coughed when something warm and wet was pressed to his lips, too tired to stop himself from swallowing whatever it was. Wasn't his life supposed to be flashing before his eyes right about now? Shouldn't he be thinking of his grandfather, who would be expecting him on Monday?

But all he could really think was *I never texted Blake back.*

"My, that was quite fast."

Cass blinked heavy eyes, trying his best to focus. Whatever room he was in—his hotel room, he had to assume—felt very, very bright, and whatever cooling or heating system they had going on was loud as all hell. Or maybe that was just the hangover talking.

But that voice didn't sound like Blake. That sounded like—who did that sound like?

"It can take days, the transformation. Some part of you must have been quite eager to return to this mortal realm, hm?"

Who the fuck talked like that? Oh, right. The guy from last night. Half-charming, half-creepy, now that Cass was thinking about it with a sober brain.

Dang it, how much had Cass had to drink last night? Too much, surely. Had they...?

But no, he didn't feel like they had. He wasn't sore. Not even his neck.

His *neck*.

"Hey!" Cass shot up in the bed. He had a vague impression they were in some fancy hotel room. Definitely not the cheap one he and Blake had rented for two nights, the one with paint chipping off the walls and carpet from some 1970s nightmare. He thought he was maybe in the hotel connected to the bar from the night before—it had the same understated elegance. But that wasn't the point. The point was...

Cass shook an accusatory finger. "Last night. You *bit* me."

The man from the night before—and had Cass really not thought to be 100 percent certain of the guy's name before agreeing to go off with him?—looked more amused than chagrined at the accusation. "Yes," he agreed. "You were quite delicious too. Almost a shame to turn you."

Cass was already busy running his hands over his body, gratified to note he was still in the same clothes he'd passed out in. "You talk a lot of nonsense, did you know that?"

That seemed to irritate his attacker, whose smirk gave way to a small frown. "Yes. Well. Let me explain some of what you're feel—"

Cass held up a hand. Something was missing. "Where's my phone?"

Now Maybe-Arthur did look taken aback, more so than when Cass had accused him of nibbling on his neck. "Excuse me?"

"My *phone*. I forgot to text Blake last night."

Maybe-Arthur silently pointed to the bedside table on the opposite side of the bed, and Cass lunged for it. He had texts. A lot of them. And missed calls. A lot of those too. Every single one of them from Blake.

"Fuck." Cass stared down at the evidence of his carelessness. "I have to go."

"That wouldn't be wise, in your current state."

"I've had a hangover before, thank you very much."

"Aren't you...hungry?" Maybe-Arthur was looking at him oddly, as if Cass was acting in some way completely unexpected. Exactly what he *had* been expecting from the college kid he'd bitten and then dragged unconscious to his hotel room, Cass had no idea.

"Starving," Cass admitted, untangling himself from the sheets. "I always am after drinking. But there's no time. Blake's worried."

He shot what he hoped was a reassuring text. *Still alive. Sorry. Be back in ten.*

"So hungry as you are, you're determined to get back to this roommate?" The guy sounded so strangely stunned about it, it was almost funny. Maybe *his* hangover was clouding his brain too.

"Yeah, I am." Although, come to think of it, Cass's hangover wasn't so bad. True, his stomach was sort of cramping a little. And his vision was weirdly sharp, which wasn't exactly a symptom he'd had before. But no headache, no nausea. Just...restlessness, like he didn't quite fit into his own skin. Like there was something *else* there with him. Something pushing at the back of his mind.

Maybe he should stay away from manhattans from now on.

"Interesting," Maybe-Arthur mused.

Interesting or not, Cass just...he needed to get back to Blake was all. The more he thought about it, the more it was all he *could* think about. It was making his skin positively itch. He could picture Blake's gorgeous black hair, the way it always fell in front of his eyes no matter how he styled it. Those perfectly bright green eyes, like no one else Cass had ever seen. And he always smelled so good, didn't he? Cass should be there with him. Maybe—maybe Blake would be so happy to see him he'd get a hug. Maybe Blake would hold him. Maybe—

A clearing throat brought him back to reality. Right, he was still in this room. With a complete stranger.

Cass cocked a hand on his hip. "You know, you really shouldn't be bringing drunk dates home like this. It's really bad form."

"Bad...form," Maybe-Arthur repeated, like Cass was speaking a foreign language.

"Yeah. Bad form. Sorry if you thought you were getting laid. But...no way."

"Right." Slowly—so slowly as to be actually entirely creepy—Maybe-Arthur's stunned expression turned into a smile. "Well, by all means, young Cassian. Go ahead. But don't say I didn't warn you. If you need me, I'll be at the same bar tonight."

Cass was already on his way out the door, visions of his reunion with Blake dancing in his head. The visions were quickly turning X-rated. Which was crazy, and should probably have been alarming. But Cass couldn't find it in himself to care, not when he was suddenly so...hungry. Hungry for one thing and one thing only. So no, he wasn't going to need this guy. He only needed one thing.

His roommate.

Two

Blake

Blake was pacing. Across—and back across and then across once again—their tiny motel room. It was maybe weird of him, since he was pretty sure he'd never paced before, had only seen it in movies. But he'd never experienced this kind of nervous restlessness before either.

Cass was missing. *Missing.*

Well, okay, he'd texted just a second ago that he was alive and he'd be back in ten minutes, but he'd *been* missing. All fucking night. Blake had barely slept at all, waking what felt like every five minutes thinking he'd heard the ding of a text or the buzz of a phone call.

Blake didn't get it. It wasn't like Cass at all. Cass could be a little absent-minded, sure, when it came to taking care of himself. He'd forget to eat breakfast or take his jacket when it was cold out. Blake had gotten used to reminding him of those little things. But when it came to other people, Cass was...thoughtful. *Sweet* was probably a better word for it, even though Blake didn't usually go around thinking of other guys as sweet. Cass always said please and thank-you to everyone, always coupled the polite words with these shy, adorable smiles no one could help responding to. He was a good communicator, never making Blake wait for a text or a call back. He didn't play stupid games.

Which was why it had already been unsettling enough the night before, when he hadn't been responding to Blake's invite out, not even to decline in that overly polite way he did sometimes.

Had the invitation itself been the problem? Had Blake scared him off with the mention of strangers? If so, Blake wanted to kick himself. He should have known better. He *did* know better. Cass had always been shy of new people. But Blake had been flush with the excitement of a great day of powder, and the three dudes he'd kept running into on the slopes had offered to buy him a beer afterward. He had thought Cass would maybe like them. One of them was even a big reader, and Cass fucking loved books. Maybe they would have hit it off. Maybe Cass would have even, like, *really* liked him...

Blake frowned, kicking softly at the motel's desk and shaking that thought from his head. He couldn't picture Cass with any of the snowboarders from yesterday. He didn't exactly want to. Not that he had any problem with Cass liking dudes the way he did. Just... It was hard to imagine the right guy for him, one who would appreciate all the little things Blake had come to appreciate, in their time rooming together. Cass stocking all the sodas Blake liked in his mini fridge, since Blake didn't have one of his own. The way he listened—really listened—in a way few of Blake's buddies ever did. The way he was the absolute best study buddy in the world, quiet and intense but always down for a late-night diner trip after, to unwind with loaded fries and milkshakes.

Blake had really lucked out, rooming with him. He had been hoping Cass would agree to it next year. And after—well, after college they'd still be friends, wouldn't they? Hell, they were both from Phoenix. They could get a bachelor pad together or something. There was no reason they couldn't keep living together for years to come.

If Cass came back, that was. Which he would. He'd said he would. He'd just really freaked Blake out was all. And Blake maybe wouldn't believe he was safe until he saw him—that shy smile, his messy hair, that cute little upturned nose he always scrunched when he found something funny, or confusing, or—

Blake was finally able to quit his pacing when the door opened. And there was Cass, looking....well, not quite like Blake had expected. He'd expected him to be sheepish—embarrassed, maybe—but he looked...

Blake didn't quite know. Cass's gray-blue eyes were bright and shining, his smattering of freckles standing out in sharp contrast to his pale face, but his cheeks were high with color.

Had he run all the way there or something?

"S-Sorry," Cass mumbled, standing statue still in the doorway. He looked almost afraid, standing there. Did he think Blake was mad at him? That he'd yell or something?

Never. Blake would *never* yell at him.

"Cass." Blake held his arms open, walking forward, hoping to coax him out of the doorway. But he didn't get far before Cass beat him to it, running into his arms at an alarming speed. Blake caught him and wrapped him up tight. They didn't hug much—what was the need, when they saw each other literally every day?—but that was a shame because hugging Cass was kind of perfect. He was small and slim, easy to get ahold of, and his head tucked perfectly under Blake's chin. They should definitely hug more. And they kind of were already because Cass wasn't letting go. He'd started rubbing his nose against Blake's chest in a way that sort of tickled, mumbling something into the fabric of Blake's T-shirt.

"What was that, buddy?"

Cass lifted his head just slightly, enough for the words to come out without creating any real distance between them. "Smell good."

Well, that definitely couldn't be true, after Blake's restless, sweaty night, but oh well, who was he to argue? Cass smelled good too. He always did. Kind of sweet, like his personality. Maybe it was his shampoo.

"Are you—did something bad happen?" Blake asked, barely daring to breathe in case the answer was yes.

"Met a guy," Cass mumbled. "At a bar."

"Oh. *Oh.*" Blake tried to think through the weird, rancid curl in his gut. He didn't need to treat this like a big deal. It wasn't. Cass could spend the night with whoever he wanted. "Did you finally lose that *V* card, buddy?" Blake tried for light and teasing, but it come out strangled.

Cass was still—well, he was either shaking his head or just trying to rub his nose into Blake's sternum. Or maybe both. "Nothing happened," he said. "Drank too much."

"And that's why you didn't text? You passed out?" The thought was kind of horrifying. Cass should know better than to get hammered with some strange dude. Anything could have happened to him. But maybe now wasn't the time to talk about that, not when Cass was clearly still out of it from whatever had happened.

"Sorry," Cass mumbled again.

"It's okay." Blake rubbed his hand up and down Cass's spine, trying to soothe him. "Just, um, try to remember next time, okay? I was pretty worried." That was maybe the understatement of the year, judging by how shaky Blake was from the sheer force of relief running through his veins. Holy fuck.

It wasn't like Blake was usually this protective of his friends. It was just... Most of the guys he knew could take care of themselves. Not that Cass couldn't, but he was just so...sweet. It would be way too easy for some creep to take advantage of him.

Blake realized they'd been hugging for what was probably a completely inappropriate amount of time, but he was still reluctant to let go. Which was probably for the best because not only was Cass not letting go, but he was now pushing Blake back with surprising strength—seriously, when had he gotten so strong?—until his knees hit the motel's desk chair.

Blake was sitting before he knew it, and then he had a lapful of Cass. Which was...new. But also...nice?

Cass fit perfectly in his lap, and he really did smell so good. "Are you sure you're okay? This guy didn't...do anything?"

"Bit me."

Blake managed to laugh through another surge of what felt an awful lot like jealousy. "Oh yeah? You got a hickey? Let me see."

But Cass still had his head buried in Blake's chest. And he was kind of...squirming. It was honestly a little distracting because his ass kept brushing against Blake's dick, and Blake may have been straight, but... Well, friction was friction, especially with a soft, sweet-smelling bundle of Cass in his arms.

"Um, buddy?" Blake said, keeping his voice soft and nonjudgmental. "We're about to have a situation if you keep moving like that. I'm only human, man."

Cass only slid himself even tighter against him, and then Blake realized they already had a situation because Cass...

Cass was hard.

Blake could feel it through the stiff material of Cass's ridiculous dress pants, pressed against his stomach. Which may have short-circuited his brain for a hot second, but who could blame him? He'd just never had another dude's hard dick pressed against him. He should be turned off, even with all the squirming.

But then Cass finally looked up at him, and... Oh, wow. His cheeks were still flushed, and his eyes had grown darker, the pupils blown wide.

He looked desperate.

And maybe that shouldn't have been doing things for Blake, but it kind of, sort of was. He could feel the blood rushing south to his dick, faster than it had any right to.

But then Cass's cute little nose was scrunching up. "I'm sorry!" he moaned. "I don't know what's wrong with me."

Blake tried to think through this new, unexpected fog of lust. "Did you, um, take something? Last night?"

"No!" Cass shook his head in agitated denial. "You just smell so good, and I'm all—I'm all—"

Blake smirked down at him. "Horny as hell?"

"Blake!" Cass whined. "It's not funny."

"I'm sorry, baby, I know it's not." The endearment sort of just slipped out, and Blake didn't have it in him to take it back. He'd meant to say "buddy," like usual.

But Cass didn't even seem to notice, and he was just looking so goddamn distraught by his own arousal that Blake couldn't help it. He shifted his hips, making Cass aware of his own...situation. "It's fine. See, baby? Everybody gets turned on sometimes."

It was a stupid fucking thing to say, but Cass seemed to grow the slightest bit calmer with his words. He was still looking desperate, his eyes boring into Blake's. "I need... I need..."

It was clear enough what he needed.

"You want my help?" Blake asked. "Want me to touch you?"

Cass nodded, looking glum. "But you're—"

Blake didn't even let him finish that sentence. Maybe he'd regret this later, when the rush of relief at Cass's reappearance had faded and he no longer had a lapful of Cass testing his self-restraint. But that was something for future Blake to deal with. "Hey, it's fine," he soothed, interrupting Cass's assertion of Blake's straightness. "What are roommates for, huh? Beats jerking off to terrible porn, right?"

Cass looked unbearably hopeful at the reassurance, staring at Blake like he was the best thing in the whole, wide world.

And who the fuck could resist *that*?

Blake moved before either of them could change their mind, unbuttoning Cass's pants and sliding his own basketball shorts down his hips until both their erections were exposed to the cool hotel-room air.

And Cass's dick...it wasn't scary at all, was it? It was kind of cute, actually. Proportionate to his size, all flushed and leaking, like just being in Blake's lap was some sort of massive turn-on. And why shouldn't it be? He was a good-looking guy. He could be a fantasy for someone like Cass, couldn't he? Better than some hotel stranger.

He looked up from his assessment to see Cass staring at Blake's dick in turn, like it was literal candy. Blake gripped himself, feeling stupidly smug. "You like that, baby?"

Cass licked at his lips. "You're very...hung."

Pride blossomed in Blake's chest. See? Cass didn't need to hook up with some small-town sleaze. He had Blake.

"Should I—?" Cass reached for his own cock, but Blake shook his head.

"I've got a better idea."

He pulled Cass closer, slotting both their cocks together and covering them with his hand. Fuck. The press of Cass's soft skin, the harsh exhale Cass let out at the contact. It was all a surprisingly heady thing.

And yeah, it was a little awkward at first, pumping them both without any lube, but Cass was a leaker, and soon Blake had a sticky-slick glide going on. And it was hotter than it had any fucking right to be. Especially when Blake looked up again to see Cass staring down, mesmerized.

Blake couldn't help it. He leaned down and kissed him. Which probably made this something more than just roomies helping roomies. It was just... Cass was super kissable was all. Even for a dude. He had surprisingly pouty lips for such a serious face, Blake had always thought. And then he couldn't help slipping his tongue in, just to see what it was like. And it was good. Really fucking good. Cass's mouth was hot and wet, and he was letting out these little moans that had Blake picking up the pace. It wasn't an experiment anymore; he was desperate now. And so was Cass, from the sound of it.

Cass broke the kiss first, panting. "Blake. I'm gonna—gonna—"

"Yeah, you can come, baby. Come all over my hand. That's fine. That's just fucking fine."

It was more than fine. Blake needed it. He needed to see what Cass looked like when he came. And it was totally worth it when he did—his mouth dropped open, his lips all bruised from Blake's kisses, and he closed his pretty eyes, his pale lashes fluttering. It was a really fucking stellar orgasm face, actually. Like, kind of beautiful.

Cass slumped against him, tucking his head into Blake's neck, whimpering from overstimulation as Blake stroked his cum over both their cocks. Blake was about to release him and get to stroking himself to the finish, but then he felt a sharp sting.

Fuck. Had Cass just *bitten* him?

That was kind of hot, actually. And then it was kind of weird. Really weird. Because tingles from the bite were traveling down Blake's body, rushing down to his cock, tightening his balls up like he was going to come any second. It felt...really fucking good. And Cass was making these strange, greedy noises. Kind of like gulping. Like he was...drinking?

But it was hard to focus when Blake's cock was emptying itself all over his hand, his cum mixing with Cass's. He hadn't even been stroking it, too startled by the bite. It had just happened, all on its own.

And then they were both panting, Blake doing his best to orient himself after the last few minutes. Cass was...licking his neck?

Blake was going to have the world's biggest hickey, wasn't he?

And at some point, Blake was going to have to process all this, but he wanted to make sure Cass was okay first. He was a sensitive guy, and it was all too likely he was going to get unreasonably embarrassed by his own neediness. So Blake tugged Cass's head back gently by the hair, reluctant as he was to pull Cass's mouth off him.

But Cass looked...different. Really different. His pupils were still blown, that was for sure, but not like normal. It was like they were everywhere, like there were no whites to his eyes at all. Like his whole fucking eyeball was black.

And between those sweet, pouty lips—the ones Blake had lost his mind kissing—Cass's teeth were longer, like he had fangs. Cute little fangs. Cute, except they were kind of red, like they were covered in blood.

Blake was pretty sure they were covered in *his* blood.

"What. The actual. Fuck."

Three

Cass

"What. The. Fuck."

Cass bit at his lip, trying to come back to his senses even a little bit. Blake was staring at him, his green eyes intense as could be. He was also panting. They were *both* panting. Because—holy freaking hell—they'd both just come, hadn't they? In Blake's hand. Together. Cass could see the evidence right now, coating Blake's stomach. But also...

Cass tried to articulate some of the madness that had just occurred. "I just drank your blood, didn't I?"

"What. The. Fuck," Blake said again.

It was the second time in less than a minute. Had Cass maybe broken his brain? Was Blake freaking out about the hooking up or the blood drinking? Probably the blood drinking. That was what they should *both* be freaking out about. Not the cum on Blake's stomach or their continuously horny thoughts.

Begone, horny thoughts, Cass ordered.

It didn't exactly work. Blake was just so handsome. And built. And he'd just worked Cass over with way more skill than he should have been able to, given his complete lack of experience with sexing up the same sex.

It wasn't like Cass had *meant* to drink Blake's blood. He'd just smelled so good, especially that tender little spot at the crook of his shoulder, and then all of a sudden Cass had been so *thirsty*. And something in him—that new, heavy presence in his head—had wanted a taste. And he'd thought he'd just...bite him. Like, a sexy bite. Just a little nibble. But when he'd leaned into Blake's neck, Cass had felt his own face, like, shift somehow, and then his teeth had just cut right through Blake's skin like freaking butter.

And now Blake was still staring. It seemed kind of pointed. Which was probably fair.

But it was enough to give a guy certain misgivings. "Do I look weird?" Cass asked, suddenly self-conscious.

"You have my blood on your mouth." Blake sounded more confused than horrified, so that was probably good. And he wasn't pushing Cass off his lap, which was a major win.

Cass licked at his lips, trying to get off the excess blood. He should probably be trying to wipe it off—that would have been more sanitary—but he didn't want to waste it. It just tasted so *good*. Like... Like... Like the hot chocolate Cass's mom had used to make around the holidays, before she'd passed away, if that hot chocolate hadn't tasted like chocolate, but copper and salt and something indescribably *Blake*.

So maybe it didn't taste like hot chocolate at all.

"Your eyes," Blake murmured, scanning Cass's face. "Your *teeth*."

Cass couldn't help it—he squirmed a little. It was just, Blake was still *staring*, in that same intense way. And he was so handsome, his green eyes all sort of heavy-lidded from leftover lust or whatever, his tanned cheeks spotted with color. It was distracting. It made Cass's skin itch again. Like he wanted to bite him again. Or be bitten. Or maybe see if that big cock could fit in his mouth.

*I said be*gone, *horny thoughts.*

Cass tried to focus on the matter at hand. He'd done something weird, even weirder than jumping his roommate like some horned-up beast. And it wasn't like he could see his own eyes, but he lifted a hand to see what Blake meant about his teeth. *Oh.* His incisors were definitely longer. Sharper.

No wonder Blake's neck had been like butter.

"Oh!" Cass held up his finger. He'd poked it accidentally, and a bead of blood was welling up. He licked it off. It didn't taste nearly as good as Blake's.

But then that was it. No more beads of blood appeared. Like Cass's finger hadn't been poked at all.

"It's healed." Cass tilted his head, studying the side of Blake's neck. "Your bite has too. I think I licked it all better."

That seemed to be the final straw for Blake, in terms of the weirdness of the morning. He shook his head forcefully, like he was clearing it of some fog, his black hair whirling around his face with the motion. "All right," he bit out. "So maybe we should put our dicks away and talk about what exactly happened to you last night."

Cass pouted a bit at that, even though it was probably a good idea. He just really liked being on Blake's lap. And he liked having their dicks touching, even if they were soft and covered with drying cum now. It was still...intimate.

Blake narrowed his eyes. "Don't look at me like that, baby. You just drank my blood like a fucking milkshake. We need to talk."

Cass perked up again at that. *Baby.* It wasn't the first time Blake had called him that either. Maybe he wouldn't be banned from the lap forever. "I'll get a washcloth," he offered, hopping off Blake and rushing into the bathroom.

He was wetting the washcloth in the sink when he finally looked up and saw what Blake had been talking about: Cass's eyes were all black. Like, no pale-blue irises, no whites to them at all. Freaky fucking demon eyes. "What the fuck" was right. It was a miracle Blake hadn't shoved him off and run out of the room.

Cass bared his teeth at his reflection. And it was exactly what it had felt like—he had a pair of legitimate fangs.

So now would probably be a good time to panic, right? Except... Blake was here. And he wasn't running, even though Cass sort of looked like a literal monster. He wanted to talk it over, even. They were going to sort it out somehow.

Cass took a deep breath and let it out slowly, then winked at his terrifying reflection, just to see. "We're going to fix this," he whispered. "It's going to be fine."

He dashed back into the room with the wet washcloths, and they both cleaned themselves up. Cass was even supergood and barely sneaked a peek at his semiexposed roommate. (Not that he hadn't gotten a good, long look earlier.)

When they were somewhat presentable, Blake sat down on the edge of one of the hotel beds, the one that was all mussed up like someone had been fighting their own sheet all night. Had he brought someone here last night? But no, Cass could only smell Blake in the room. And he didn't really want to focus on how freaky it was that he could tell that by scent alone, so he pushed it out of his mind.

Cass considered sitting on the other bed, but that seemed...wrong. And it would be too weird to climb up onto Blake's lap again, right? He couldn't bring himself to go too far away though. Something in him still felt like it needed to be very, very close to Blake.

He sat next to Blake on the foot of the used bed.

It wasn't good enough.

So Cass sidled closer, trying to get near enough that their arms brushed, without seeming too obvious about it.

Blake let out a huff of a laugh, immediately catching on. "Needy little thing today, aren't you?" But he sounded more fond than frustrated. And then he did the best thing *ever*. He put his arm around Cass's shoulders and tucked him in close. "Tell me everything that happened last night."

Cass did another one of his slow, deep breaths—his therapist would be so freaking proud—and then he did. Blake listened carefully. He always had, though, even when Cass was going off about something that was probably mind-numbingly boring to anyone else, like the world-building details of one of his favorite video games.

He tightened his hold ever so slightly when Cass got to the part about agreeing to go home with the guy, but he never interrupted. Not until Cass had filled him in on every detail up to returning to the hotel room and jumping his bones.

"Okay. So." Blake cleared his throat. "He bit you in that alley. Drank your blood, maybe. You passed out after he slipped you something."

"I was *already* passing out when he fed me whatever," Cass corrected.

"Okay, you were *already* passing out. Then you woke up in his room, unharmed as far as you could tell. And you started...craving me."

Cass nodded, his head brushing against Blake's soft T-shirt. "Yep."

He felt more than heard Blake's sigh, his whole body seeming to expand with the motion. "Okay. All right. Do you remember how to get to his hotel room?"

Cass frowned in thought. "I think so."

"And do you think you can make your face...um...go back to how it was?"

That was the question, wasn't it? "I don't know," Cass admitted.

Blake leaned back, enough to look Cass in the eye. "How did you change it in the first place?"

"I have no idea!" Cass's frustration came out in a whine. "I was just...thirsty. And you smelled so good, and I got all excited. And I just changed."

It had been a little stranger than that, what with this new presence inside him, one that itched to come out when Blake was near. But Cass didn't want to freak Blake out any more than he needed to, so he kept that little bit to himself for now.

"Okay, so... Try to relax again." Blake petted Cass's hair, apparently thinking that was the key to relaxing him.

It did honestly feel pretty nice. So Cass tried. But Blake still smelled really good. And Cass was still kind of horny even though he'd just come ten minutes ago. So he tried to bargain inside his own head instead.

Hey...thing inside me. You can chill out now. We aren't thirsty anymore. We drank, and we're all good. So go back to where you came from.

Maybe he was crazy trying to negotiate with some intangible presence, but it wasn't long before Cass heard what almost sounded like a weird inner grumble and then felt a shift.

He held a hand up to his teeth, feeling around his incisors. They felt normal again.

And Blake was beaming down at him, like Cass had just aced some impossible exam. "Good job, buddy. Really good job. Now let's go talk to this creep."

"Excuse me?" Cass frowned up at him, irritated by either the "buddy" or the suggestion itself; he wasn't actually sure.

"For all we know, he slipped you some never-heard-of party drug that...makes you crave blood and get all horny or...fuck, I don't know." Blake stopped at Cass's pitiful look, rubbing at his shoulder in some semblance of reassurance. "He'll have answers, won't he?"

"Maybe..."

The truth was Cass didn't want Blake anywhere near the creep from last night. But Blake was looking so hopeful that they'd find some sort of solution. And he still wasn't running, was he? He was staying by Cass's side. So Cass pulled on his metaphorical big-boy pants and stood up, straightening his button-down. "Okay. Yeah. Let's do this."

They pulled up to the hotel some twenty minutes later, walking into the lobby like they both belonged there. No one tried to stop them or ask for a room key, so Cass headed straight for the elevators, pressing what he was 90 percent sure was the right button. He didn't tell Blake that while he remembered which floor he'd been on, he didn't remember the room number itself.

It was just... He could sort of track the guy's scent? And that felt too weird to admit out loud.

Maybe-Arthur hadn't smelled good in the way Blake did, but it had still been distinctive—kind of metallic, even. A scent Cass was learning to associate with blood.

When he found what he hoped was the right room, he paused in spite of himself, and Blake ended up knocking on the door for him, more forcefully than Cass would have. And then he stood real close, right next to Cass, with his arms crossed like some kind of club bouncer.

He was trying to be intimidating. Succeeding, really, as far as Cass was concerned, given his muscular frame and impressive height. It was protective. Sweet, even. He'd been nothing *but* sweet since the moment Cass had barged into the room, practically accosting him with the force of his horniness.

It honestly made Cass want to throw his head back and groan. Because *why* did Blake have to be so sweet all the time? If the world worked the way it was supposed to, he should have been, like, some absent-mindedly cruel jock type. That would have been easy enough to ignore, no matter how good-looking he was. But how the hell was Cass going to get over this crush now, when he knew the husky groan Blake let out when he came, the way his eyes grew hot and heavy with lust when he was turned on?

And he *had* been turned on. By Cass, against all odds. so maybe he wasn't 100 percent, all-the-way, for-sure straight. Maybe there was a little wiggle room where Cass could slip in and be held and called "baby" in that soft way.

Maybe—

The hotel door opened, and there was the man from last night, smirking at Cass like he'd been expecting him. "You came back. I knew you woul—" He seemed to finally notice that Cass had a shadow, doing a little a double take at Blake's impressive glare before smirking again. "And you brought a snack for us."

Blake puffed up noticeably. "Listen, pal—" Cass tried to suppress a snort. It wasn't the time, but he'd never heard Blake say anything so cliché in their entire time together, and it was honestly a little hilarious. "We want answers," Blake continued, undeterred. "What the hell did you do to my friend last night?"

"The infamous Blake, I presume." The bar creep looked him over slowly, not seeming a bit intimidated, even though Blake had multiple inches and some number of pounds on him.

Jesus. Had Cass really talked about him that much in his tipsy state? He could feel his face heating as Blake shot him a surprised glance before turning his full ire back to the room's inhabitant. "We could have you arrested, you know."

Maybe-Arthur—and Cass *really* wished he had gotten the guy's actual name— sighed heavily, like they were putting him out beyond belief. "All right. Come in. Let's get the interrogation over with. But it'll have to be quick."

It looked like they had come just in time, because the man's bag was on the bed, looking close to completely packed. Had he been about to run out? Or had he been waiting for Cass to come back first?

Blake wasted no time. "What did you do to Cass?

"I fed from him, then I turned him," Maybe-Arthur said, shrugging a casual shoulder like his answer was completely obvious.

Cass fought the urge to roll his eyes. *Great clarification, Maybe-Arthur.*

Blake made a frustrated sound. "Turned him...how?"

"With my blood." It might have been Cass's imagination, but Maybe-Arthur seemed almost amused at Blake's confusion. Was he just toying with them?

"Into *what*?" Blake asked, patience clearly wearing thin.

Maybe-Arthur cocked a brow. "Why, a vampire, of course. What else? I'm assuming he's already fed from you? You have that look about you."

"That's—but—vampires aren't *real.*"

"I assure you, they are."

The two of them had a staring standoff then, Maybe-Arthur still looking sardonically amused and Blake looking like maybe he was going to start throwing fists and asking questions later. Cass had a feeling they weren't going to get very far with the two of them at each other's throats—especially if one of them came with a pair of unnaturally sharp teeth—so he inserted himself between them. "Can you tell me *why* you turned me?" he asked.

"Oh." Maybe-Arthur shrugged, his coy smile dropping. "Well, you were so sad. And awfully cute. I'm afraid I was a little impulsive. It seemed like a good idea at the time. You and I could have had a bit of fun." He shot an annoyed glance at Blake. "But it seems you already have your tether."

"My tether," Cass repeated.

"Yes. Lucky you."

"What's a tether?" Blake asked, sounding put out to be left out of the conversation.

"Yes, Arthur, what's a tether?"

Maybe-Arthur looked at Cass blankly. "Arthur?"

"Is that...not your name?"

"This whole time you thought my name was *Arthur*?" Definitely-Not-Arthur looked properly upset for the first time in that entire interaction, but then he huffed a sigh. "Look, as adorable as your newbie vamp cluelessness is, I'm afraid I simply don't have the time," he said, stepping briefly into the bathroom and returning with pilfered toiletries he stuffed into his bag. It was a surprisingly mundane act for someone claiming to be undead. "I was mistaken. This isn't free territory, which means I need to go. And you'd be wise to do the same."

He grabbed his packed bag, moving to step out of the room. Blake—foolish, loyal Blake—stepped in front of him, probably hoping to block him, but then Not-Arthur's face changed, just like Cass's had: his eyes turned black, his fangs dropped, and he did a weird...growl thing.

Could Cass *growl* now?

Blake stepped back, clearly thrown by the change, and Not-Arthur took advantage of his shock and fled the room, faster than should have been possible.

And then there were two.

"So... I'm a vampire," Cass said brightly, trying to smile in some sort of carefree, reassuring way. He was pretty sure he just looked constipated.

Blake frowned at him. "We're not going to take that creep's word on it."

So they were still going the denial route. Cass sighed, fake smile dropping. "Oh yeah? Then what, Blake?"

"We're taking you to the hospital."

"Jesus." Cass rubbed his hands over his face. "I'm gonna end up in the psych ward."

But then Blake was there, hugging him tight, rubbing his hand up and down Cass's spine in reassurance. "Not if you *show* them. I'm not going to let anything bad happen to you. I promise. I've got your back."

And how could Cass argue with that?

Four

Blake

Blake flipped through the rumpled magazine, scanning the images without reading any of the words. They'd been waiting a few hours already in the small emergency room waiting room. Blake had heard somewhere that abdominal pain got you bumped up the line, so he'd coached Cass on what to say and told him to at least try to look like he was uncomfortable, but it didn't seem to be getting them seen any faster.

The boredom of waiting was somewhat improved by the fact that Cass's version of pretending to be in pain seemed to be curling up into Blake in the waiting room chair, tucking his head into Blake's shoulder like a little kitten. It shouldn't have made the wait better, really. Blake had only one serious relationship under his belt, and she'd been way too into PDA and physical contact in general: always clinging to his arm, wanting to hold his hand, or snuggling into him in public. He'd tried to resign himself to it to make her happy, but he'd hated it. It had always seemed like she was trying to show him off, make a big display, like it wasn't out of any real need to connect with him. He hadn't exactly been heartbroken when she'd broken it off.

But for some reason, with Cass, he didn't mind. It was even nice. Cass smelled good, especially when Blake pushed his nose against his soft hair. And Cass seemed to...need it, in a way. It wasn't for show, not like Blake's ex-girlfriend. He *needed* to be touching Blake, to take comfort in it.

Why didn't that bother Blake more? Because Cass was a friend, not a boyfriend? Yeah, maybe that was it—a friend in need.

A friend you jerked off this morning with more enthusiasm than you've ever shown a hookup before?

Blake ignored that unhelpful thought. There would be time for a sexuality freak-out later. Maybe. Hopefully. First, they were going to get some medical attention. They were going to get to the bottom of what was going on, an explanation that didn't include the word *vampire*. And then they were going to be fine.

Cass was going to be fine.

And *then* there'd be time to talk about the touching and the kissing and how good it had all felt.

When Cass's name was finally called, Blake had almost dozed off, his head resting on top of Cass's, Cass's hands gripping at his arm. They followed an unsmiling blonde woman into a small, curtained-off emergency bay, where she left them with instructions to wait for the nurse.

Two minutes later a guy in scrubs came in, smiling warmly at them both. He was good-looking, almost pretty, with big brown eyes and messy brown curls, a smattering of freckles that sort of matched Cass's. Jesus. Was this what Blake was doing now, noticing when guys were pretty?

"Hi, you two, I'm Danny. I'll be your nurse today." Danny turned his focus immediately on Cass. "You're Cassian?" At Cass's nod, he glanced to Blake. "And you are...?"

"I'm Blake."

"Family?"

"Boyfriend." Blake ignored the way Cass startled at his answer. Cass was already clinging to him like they were together, and Blake didn't want to be asked to leave. Boyfriend was more official than friend, right?

Danny nodded easily. "Okay. Cassian, if you're willing to release your beau and hop up on the gurney? I promise I don't bite." He smiled to himself like it was an inside joke while he pulled on a pair of blue hospital gloves.

Once Cass was on the gurney, Danny started looking him over, listening to his heart and lungs and palpating his abdomen. "Where exactly do you hurt?"

"Um..." Cass flushed at the scrutiny, clearly unsure of what to say.

"Look, sorry for lying," Blake cut in. "But we're not actually here for stomach pain. He was given something last night, and he's been having...weird symptoms ever since."

Danny leaned back from his inspection, gloved hands going to his hips. "Oh! Okay, lying to your healthcare team, always a good start." But he wasn't looking at them too harshly, despite the sarcasm—maybe ER nurses were used to getting the runaround every now and then. "Let's start with some vitals, then you can tell me about your symptoms, okay, Cassian?"

"Just Cass, please," Cass requested meekly, but Blake didn't miss the look of relief that they were no longer having to pretend.

Danny hooked Cass up to the monitor, pursing his lips while he looked it over. "Heart rate in the fifties, a little low but not unusual. You a runner, Cass?"

Cass shook his head. "Confirmed bookworm."

"Blood pressure a perfect 120 over eighty. Oxygen shows...zero percent." Danny's dark brows rose. "Huh. This cord must be broken. Feeling short of breath?"

Apparently that relief had been short-lived because Cass was fidgeting more the longer Danny spoke to him. Before Blake could reassure him with a wink or a soft touch, Cass was blurting out, unnaturally loud, "Have you ever had any vampires come through here?"

Danny stared at him.

"Like, sprouting fangs and drinking their friend's blood after a wild night out?"

Danny continued to stare for a long moment. Then he snapped his gloves off, shaking his head, and poked it out of the curtain. "Chloe, we're gonna need the isolation room!"

Without another word, he transferred them both to a real room instead of an open bay, one with sliding glass doors. He pulled a curtain over the doors so they were cut off completely from the rest of the ER. "Sorry, just...more privacy." He turned back to Cass, who he'd placed on the edge of another gurney. "All right, what exactly were you given last night?"

"Blood, I think?"

Danny bit at his lip. "After someone bit you?"

Cass nodded.

"Show me," Danny ordered.

Before Blake could ask what exactly Cass was supposed to be showing, Cass did the whole face thing again: black eyes, little fangs peeking between pink lips. It was even more disconcerting under the bright hospital fluorescents than it had been in their hotel room. Not scary, just...different.

"Okay. Well." Danny took a minute, studying them with a furrowed brow, and then out of nowhere, he was smiling warmly at them both. "Welcome to the club, then."

There was a long silence after that, with Danny still smiling like they'd just signed up for some exclusive membership.

It was Cass who found his words first, his face back to normal, clearing his throat timidly. "You, um...believe me?"

The hopeful hesitance in his voice just about gutted Blake. Had his denial over the whole thing been hurting Cass? He hadn't meant to make him feel alone. It was just... Who believed vampires were real based on the words of some hotel creep? Hadn't Blake been doing his part as a—as a *friend*—making sure they weren't letting some strange guy's lunacy become contagious?

"Of course I believe you," Danny said calmly. "You're not the only vampire in Hyde Park, you know. Brave of you to come to the hospital with it though."

"Well, Blake thought—" Cass was avoiding Blake's eyes as he spoke, and Blake suddenly missed when they'd been huddled together in the emergency room, two against the world. "He thought it might be something else."

"I'm guessing you didn't know about our kind before last night?"

Cass shook his head. "Nuh-uh."

Danny's big brown eyes filled with sympathy. "Oh God, you poor baby. Okay. Tell me everything that happened to you."

Cass did, explaining the events leading up to their ER visit, glossing over some of the steamy bits of the morning, although not enough to keep them both from blushing. When he reached the hotel creep's insistence on the "tether" part, Danny glanced over to Blake with a knowing look.

When Cass was fully done, Danny took a moment, seeming to collect his thoughts. "Okay. Wow. And you're sure this vamp left town?"

"He seemed pretty eager to go."

Danny nodded thoughtfully. "That's one problem solved. So... Man, where to start? Some vampire basics, I guess. A lot of the myths are...myths. Sunlight doesn't hurt you, as you clearly already know. Same with garlic and crosses and all that jazz. Some other stuff is true: you won't age. You won't die unless killed, and that's pretty hard to do. You have to drink blood to survive, usually about once a week, but you might need more at first while you're new. Newbie vampires tend to be...hungry." He looked between Cass and Blake again. "They also tend to be unstable. More aggressive. They have a harder time ending a feed. But you did feed? On Blake?"

Cass nodded, looking mesmerized by the words coming out of Danny's mouth. It was enough for Blake to feel an inappropriate stab of jealousy. *He* was supposed to be the one helping Cass.

Still, Blake could feel his face heating at the memory of that feed, jealousy fading. Danny glanced at him knowingly. "I bet that was fun. Vampire bites tend to be very...pleasant...for the human."

"I didn't have any trouble stopping." Cass's lips formed a small pout. "I don't think I hurt him."

"You wouldn't, I don't think," Danny said. "Not if he's your tether."

Blake finally found his voice to ask, "What is that? The other vam—the other guy said it too."

"All vampires have a mate, one that tethers you securely to your humanity. Fated, we think. Your inner vampire, that presence you feel inside you? The one hungry for blood?" Cass nodded back at him like he knew exactly what Danny was talking about. "It recognizes them. *Craves* them. Vampires who never find them tend to lose hold of their humanity. They go feral and have to be put down."

Cass cocked his head, the same way he did when he was considering some piece of complex data during one of their study sessions. "But I'll still lose him eventually, won't I? If I never age, or die, and he's human..."

Blake felt like their words were coming from very far away all of a sudden, and not only because Cass was talking about his inconvenient mortality. Because, what, now he was not just not so straight but also possibly fated *mates*? With Cass?

"Well, most mates don't stay human." Danny continued his education, he and Cass both oblivious to Blake's inner freak-out. "They're turned. The bond isn't even solidified until they are. It's actually pretty cool that he's stabilizing you even while human. I can't wait to tell the others."

They kept chatting, their words occasionally piercing through Blake's new brain fog. Danny was telling Cass something about his new ability to do compulsion, something that sounded an awful lot like mind control.

Blake stared at Cass while they spoke. He looked so...adorable. Not like something that needed human blood to survive; that was for sure. His pale-blue eyes were wide, taking in all that information, and his freckles stood out under the bright hospital lights. He seemed to be taking it shockingly well. But then, he didn't have a choice, did he? He'd been changed forever. For *literal* ever, if this nurse was to be believed. And that could be Blake too.

Most mates don't stay human.

Blake was jumping up from his seat before he knew it. "Um, Cass? I'm gonna... I'll meet you at the hotel. I need to grab some food. Human food. Feeling a bit off, you know?"

Cass and Danny looked up at him in surprise. "We've got Jell-O, or sandwiches?" Danny offered.

Blake shook his head, backing up to the glass doors. "No, I need something, like, hot. Something real. I'll—I'll see you later?"

He tried not to notice how devastated Cass looked, way more devastated than when Danny had told him he was a for-real vampire. Danny for his part looked as kind as ever but...knowing. Way too knowing. "I can make sure Cass makes it back okay," he reassured Blake.

"Thanks." Blake was already opening the sliding door. "Thank you. See you later, buddy."

Five

Cass

"**B**uddy."

It rang through the air as Blake made his hasty exit. Cass wasn't "baby" anymore, then. Back to good ol' "buddy." Should he really be surprised? A gay identity crisis was inevitable, wasn't it? Even without all the vampire stuff added to it.

Vampire.

Cass should be the one freaking out, not Blake. He'd just found out his entire existence was forever changed. Except... He'd already gulped down Blake's blood like jungle juice at a frat party. It was hard to be in proper denial after that, no matter how much he'd wanted to placate Blake by going to the ER in the first place.

He realized Danny was looking at him with something awfully akin to pity in his eyes. Cass straightened his back, trying to exude less of a pathetic vibe. "I guess the 'fleeing from my side' part of that exit was pretty obvious, huh?"

Danny winced in sympathy. "Just a little. This thing between you two is pretty new, huh?"

"As new as being a vampire is," Cass admitted. "Blake's straight. He's not really my boyfriend; he's my roommate."

"Oh. Well, damn." Danny's eyes widened in understanding. "That's a lot at once, isn't it?"

"Tell me about it."

Danny took a seat on a stool to the right of the gurney. "You're awfully cool about the supernatural part of this, you know. Have you thought about what it means? Never aging? What you're going to tell your family?"

"Oh, it's just me and my grandpa. I'm not sure he'll be around long enough to notice." Cass felt a sharp pang at the thought, but it was a reality he'd come to terms with a long time ago. "Anything else I need to know before I head out?"

"I'll give you my number." Danny reached out a hand. "I'm sure a lot will come up."

Cass gave him his phone without a fuss, watching as he punched his phone number in. For the first time since this whole ordeal had started, he was feeling truly...low.

Danny looked up from the phone knowingly. "You miss him already, don't you?"

Cass held back a sigh. "That's weird, isn't it?"

"For normal people, maybe... For mates?" Danny shrugged. "Not weird at all. He's probably missing you too."

"I doubt that. Straight, remember?"

Danny bit at his lower lip, seemingly conflicted. "Not to speak for someone else, especially with something as complicated as sexuality can be, but... I've known several fated pairs at this point. It never seems to be wrong, no matter how unlikely it looks in the beginning. So...I'm guessing Blake is at least a little..."

"Curious?" Cass asked, trying not to sound bitter.

"I can also see the way he looks at you. That's more than just a bromance, I'd say."

"Good thing. I'm not much of a bro."

Danny smiled at that. "Me neither. Now let's get you out of here before a doctor finally comes by to check you out. I'm telling them you left against medical advice, so... Apologies for the stain on your medical reputation."

Cass left the emergency room with a new paper bag, one containing what felt like a conspicuous blood bag Danny had given him to tide him over in case he got hungry again while Blake was gone, figuring himself out. Danny had even ordered him a taxi to the hotel, insisting that he not be out walking around on his own after the revelations of the day.

When he made it back to the hotel room, Cass flung the paper bag into the mini fridge, then sat heavily on one of the beds, the neatly made one he hadn't slept in the night before. Blake's bed was still a mess. It always was, back in their dorm room. Cass never minded; he had kind of always thought it made the place feel cozy.

But then again, that was just Blake. Making Cass feel warm and welcome, no matter how different they could be.

There'd been one day early into fall semester. Cass had done horribly on a test, for a prerequisite class he needed to graduate but had zero interest in. He'd been disappointed in himself, plus scared about the risk to his scholarship. He'd come home, and Blake had been watching a movie on his laptop in bed.

Cass had been...not disappointed to see him, exactly—he never minded having Blake around, looking all gorgeous and smiling nicely at him—but a little nervous. They'd only been rooming together a few months at that point, and Cass hadn't been quite ready to have a full-fledged emotional breakdown in front of him.

But Blake had taken one look at his face, patted the bed with one hand, and ordered him to hop on up and watch the movie with him. Cass had curled up next to him, leaving plenty of space, afraid to accidentally touch, and Blake had immediately put an arm around him, pulling him close enough to see the screen.

After several minutes of holding his breath, afraid to be thought of as enjoying it too much, Cass had finally given in and asked, "You know I'm gay, right?"

He hadn't exactly been in the closet, but it wasn't something the two of them had ever talked about either.

"Oh yeah," Blake had said, not taking his eyes off the movie. "Or at least, I thought. All those rainbow stickers on your laptop." Then Blake had frowned down at him. "Why, am I making you uncomfortable?"

"No!" Cass had almost laughed out loud at the thought. "Just... *You're* not uncomfortable?"

"Nah." Blake had shrugged, looking back to their movie. "It's kind of nice. Not a lot of chances to cuddle with dude friends, right?"

Cass had finally relaxed, and they'd both watched the movie in comfortable silence until Blake had broken it. "You okay?" he had asked. "Something happen?"

"Just a bad test."

"Oh, man, I've had lots of those." Blake had chuckled, rubbing Cass's arm soothingly. "It'll be fine; it's still early in the semester. We could start studying together, if you want. Keep each other on track."

"Really?"

"Sure. I got your back, buddy. What else are roomies for?"

And that had been all it had taken for Cass to fall a little bit in love. He'd known before then that Blake was hot, sure, but that had been the first time he'd realized how fucking sweet he could be.

But there was a big difference between helping someone cheer up after a bad test and being their destined vampire mate, wasn't there? Like, Jesus.

Cass rubbed at his chest, trying to ease the ache that had formed ever since Blake had fled that ER room. He needed to let Blake go, didn't he? He couldn't ask him to turn, to give up his whole human future. And maybe—maybe Blake would be willing to stay roommates for the rest of the year, while Cass stabilized, if Cass promised to keep his hands to himself. Just so he wouldn't have to run into the woods, protecting society from himself or whatever.

Cass stared over at the mini fridge, the one holding the blood bag he was going to need to drink at some point. The evidence of exactly how not normal he was now.

Was even staying roommates too much to ask?

That new presence inside him shifted uneasily. It didn't seem to like the thought of Blake leaving their side.

Too bad, vampire brain. We're going to do the right thing. Which is whatever Blake wants. Got it?

There was no answer, just a strange gnawing in Cass's gut, one he didn't think had anything to do with hunger.

Blake

Blake bit into his burger, huddled on the tiny round picnic table outside the fast-food restaurant. It should have been mediocre, but at the moment, it was beyond good. He'd barely eaten today, and he wasn't usually known for skimping on meals. It made the burger taste like literal heaven.

Was this how Blake's blood had tasted to Cass? Juicy and delicious and satisfying on some soul-deep level? He'd certainly sounded like it, back at their hotel room—those greedy little gulping noises Cass had made while Blake had been busy coming all over his own fist.

Huh. Blake had never thought of himself as a delicious hamburger. Although, Blake's burger eating had never exactly been a sensual experience before, and Cass's feeding from him had felt anything but platonic.

Blake took another bite, nodding a greeting to the couple taking a seat at the table next to him. They were braving the early spring chill as well, dressed in puffy jackets similar to his own. Cass hadn't been dressed for the chill though. Fuck, Blake should have left him his jacket back at the hospital.

Did vampires feel cold? Was Cass even going to need Blake to look out for him anymore? According to Danny, Cass only had to feed once a week. It wasn't like he was going to need Blake reminding him to eat breakfast every morning.

And why do you need to be needed by him?

Blake bit another hunk of his burger instead of answering his own question. He didn't need a reason. He'd just felt...protective of Cass, ever since their first meeting.

Blake had stumbled into his new dorm room, carrying way too many bags at once, and Cass had already been there, perched on the side of his bed, his back ramrod straight with impeccable posture, typing away at his laptop. He'd gone full deer in headlights at Blake's entrance, and then when Blake had smiled and introduced himself, a pink flush had stolen over his cheeks, highlighting his freckles.

Blake had immediately clocked the flush, and the number of rainbow pride stickers on the little cutie's laptop, and had realized his new roommate might be very much into dudes. Cool enough, considering so was Blake's little brother, Toby. Not that Blake could have really imagined Toby at a raging party school like theirs, but maybe this Cassian guy (as he'd been named on the school's dorm assignment form) had some hidden depths.

When Cass hadn't spoken right away, Blake had prompted, "Cassian, right? I'm Blake."

"Oh, just Cass. I'm your new roommate." Cass had shrugged apologetically. "Sorry."

Blake had frowned at that, dropping his bags on the other bed. "Sorry?"

Cass's flush had deepened. "Just—I'm not—I can be..." He had looked down at his laptop, seemingly unable to meet Blake's eyes. "I'm kind of a nerd."

It wasn't like Blake hadn't gotten that vibe already, even from the two seconds they'd interacted, but he'd reassured Cass anyway. "That's cool, man. I need to get my own grades up." At Cass's suspicious look, Blake had only laughed. "I'm not going to be asking to copy your papers or anything. Just... Maybe you'll be a good influence. Rub off on me or something."

And then that blush had *really* deepened, to an almost alarming degree. Blake had tried to ignore it, to keep the good vibes going. He hadn't wanted to tease the guy. "Roomies need to have each other's backs, right?"

And that had seemed to be the right thing to say, because Cass had finally smiled—really smiled—and...*something*...had swept over Blake in that instant. Some strange protectiveness, some new need to keep this assigned roommate safe and happy.

"Right," Cass had chirped, beaming away, oblivious to the internal transformation taking place in Blake at that moment.

Blake had told himself at the time that it had been because Cass reminded him of Toby. But really, the two were nothing alike, besides an attraction to dudes.

Toby was bigger even than Blake, and an absolute menace on the lacrosse field. He wasn't small or bookish or shy or sweet. And Blake's family may have been affectionate, but they didn't sniff one another's hair or watch movies cuddled up together in bed, did they?

Fuck, had Blake had a crush on Cass this whole fucking time?

He finished up his burger in two more bites, crumpling up the wrapper as he nodded goodbye to the couple. They looked cozy, huddled up together on the bench, sharing a bag of fries.

He could picture him and Cass like that, easy. But could Cass even eat human food? Blake should have stuck around to find out, to ask Danny more questions. He shouldn't have run, shouldn't have left Cass alone with such a heavy revelation on his shoulders.

He found himself walking back in the direction of the hospital, just five minutes away from where he'd been eating. But once he got there, he only lurked outside. Cass was probably back at the hotel by now. What was Blake even thinking, coming back?

He turned on his heel and walked back, ready to march the long blocks back to the hotel. He'd use the time it took to think of what to say. An apology, for sure. But what next? What did someone say to the dude fate had apparently picked as his forever mate without even asking for either of their say-so?

"Boo!"

Blake jumped at the sound before he could stop himself. He was already on edge, okay? It had been a stressful goddamn day.

But when he turned around to tell off whoever had decided it would be hilarious to stand on street corners and scare the pants off strangers, Danny was standing there, a grey-and-blue mutt-looking dog on a leash.

"Danny. Is Cass...?"

"Back at the hotel by now. He fled shortly after you did. Never fun to be on the other side of a straight-boy freak-out, I've found," Danny said, his slight smile offsetting the harshness of his words.

"I'm not." Blake bent down to pat the dog, who was sitting obediently at his owner's side, looking up at Danny like he hung the moon.

"Not freaking out?" Danny asked, the skepticism in his voice clear enough.

"Not straight," Blake clarified, willing himself not to flush as he did so. He was getting as bad as Cass with the blushing. "I mean... I liked hooking up with him, I'm not denying that. I'm probably bi, or pan, or however people describe it when they maybe like both or all of it or whatever." He scratched a spot under the dog's chin that got the little guy's tail thumping. "I can label it later."

Danny gave him a genuine smile then, looking almost proud. "Ah. My bad, then. You just had freak-out face when you left."

"Well, there's 'I'm probably bi,' and there's 'you have a mate for all eternity, and also you have to be a vampire at some point.'"

"You know you don't *have* to be anything," Danny pointed out. "Free will still exists."

"I'm not going to abandon Cass." Blake's voice came out harsher than he intended.

"I didn't think you would," Danny said mildly. "I'm just saying... Mates may be endgame, but you don't have to start at the end. Why not start with trying to be boyfriends? But like, for real, not just for lying to hospital personnel."

Blake straightened from his crouch. Boyfriends. That didn't sound half as scary. He pictured their now-familiar tradition of movies in bed, except this time he could kiss Cass whenever he wanted, anytime Cass said something too cute to handle, like listing the reasons the sci-fi movie they were watching had just broken the laws of physics. Blake could rub Cass's back, kiss his neck, not worry about popping some inopportune hard-on he told himself was reflexive because hey, those would be expected. He'd be cuddling with his *boyfriend*.

And they'd be like that couple at the fast-food place, arms around each other, sharing a plate of fries...

"Hey, can Cass still eat french fries?"

Danny's eyes widened at the non sequitur. "As long as he gets enough blood, he can eat whatever he wants. His body pretty much functions like usual."

Blake felt like a weight had just fallen off his shoulders. "Chill." He gave the dog one last pat for good measure. "Okay, I'm off. Gonna ask Cass to be my boyfriend."

"It was that easy, huh? I barely had to talk you off the ledge at all."

Blake shrugged. "Yeah, I guess I'm pretty simple. Always have been. Kind of boring, actually. But Cass doesn't seem to mind."

Danny had a small smile on his face. "No, I'd say he doesn't."

Six

Cass

C ass was changing into fresh pajamas when he heard the sound of the hotel lock disengaging.

He'd tried to occupy himself until Blake's hopeful return as best he could, showering and straightening up his duffel, keeping his phone across the room so he wouldn't be tempted to send some sort of pathetic text.

That itchy, restless feeling had come back, the one that had led to him running to Blake in the first place that morning (and had it really only been that morning?).

But as Blake appeared in the doorway, looking tired but unfairly beautiful as always, his black hair disheveled and his green eyes shining, smelling like home, everything in Cass eased. He had to physically hold himself back from flinging his body into Blake's arms like some sort of movie damsel. He was going to be *mature*, damn it. Selfless, even.

"Hey, buddy." Blake was staring at him intensely, more intensely than he had when Cass had literally transformed into a vampire right in front of him. Was he worried Cass would bite again?

"Hello, Blake." See? Super mature. *Hey*s were for kids. Hellos were for grown adults, making grown adult sacrifices, like not getting on their knees and begging Blake to stay with them forever.

"How are you feeling?"

Cass shrugged a shoulder. "Fine. Good, even. I'm not tired at all. Or hungry. Danny gave me some extra blood though, just in case." He winced as those last words came out of his mouth. Was it too much, to be talking about drinking blood? Was he skeeving Blake out?

But Blake was nodding along like they were discussing Chinese takeout. "Good. That's good."

There was an awkward silence then, as they stood facing each other. It was hard not to step closer, hard not to try to breathe Blake in. Fuck. It was going to be more difficult than he'd thought, wasn't it? Keeping away from Blake? But he *had* to.

Cass was just opening his mouth to say so, to tell Blake he didn't have to do anything he didn't want, when Blake spoke first. "I want to start as boyfriends."

Cass stood there, his brain trying its best to catch up to the words he'd just heard. "Um..."

"I'm not saying that's, you know, endgame. But it's what I need to start with. Boyfriends first."

Cass shook his head. "No, that's not—"

"No?" Blake sounded almost devastated. "You can't want to—what—turn me this instant?"

"*What*?" What kind of a bloodthirsty beast did Blake think he was? "No. I mean no to...you know."

"No to boyfriends?" Blake asked, sounding no less devastated. "You don't like me? I thought you liked me."

Cass was beginning to think he'd slipped into a different dimension somewhere between the shower and getting dressed, one where Blake had been the one with the fierce monthslong crush and Cass was somehow the guy rejecting him. "Of course I like you," he said, trying not to laugh at the absurdity. "*You* don't like *me*."

Blake frowned at him. "I don't?"

"No, you're just...you're taking care of me. That's what you do. You're sweet and supportive of your friends, but you don't—"

Blake stepped forward, a strange smile on his face. "I'm not though."

"What?"

"I'm not usually any of those things. I'm pretty selfish, actually. Kind of a dick, even. Same with most of my friends. I'm sweet with you. Only you."

"Well..." But Cass didn't actually know what to say to that. Blake just kept stepping closer, and he smelled so good. Cass could even hear Blake's heart pounding, which was kind of wild. Was it Cass making it pound like that?

"I'm like that with you," Blake went on, his voice deepening with each word. "Because of how I feel about you."

Cass had to resist retreating backward, even though he wanted nothing more than to step forward, meet Blake in the middle. He was afraid of exactly how *much* he wanted that. "How—how do you feel about me?

"I like you," Blake said, stripping off his puffy jacket and throwing it on the hotel carpet. "I like spending time with you. I like having you in my life. And I liked touching and kissing you today—I liked that a lot. I even think there's a very good possibility I could love you, if we ever gave it a chance."

"Oh." The word left Cass like a sigh.

"Yes." Blake's lips quirked up. "Oh."

This was maybe the nicest confession in the world. And it was happening to *Cass*. The trouble was it was becoming hard to focus because Blake was pretty much in touching distance now, and Cass was getting distracted. That itchy, restless presence didn't understand why they weren't already touching him, licking him, biting him. It wasn't even hungry, Cass didn't think; it just wanted more of Blake.

Blake cocked his head. "Cass?"

"Sorry, it's just...the new vampire thing. Danny told me we can get really, um, horny? For our ma—for our *boyfriends*," he corrected.

And there, that had to be the least nice confession in the world, didn't it? Blake had said all that lovely stuff about liking him, and Cass had just told him he was a mindless, horny beast.

But Blake was smiling at him fully now, all tender lips and heated eyes. "Well, I guess these new vamps' boyfriends better take good care of them, then, huh?"

"Huh?" That was the best Cass could articulate. Because now Blake was pressed against him, so close that Cass had to lift his head to look at him, and Cass had the brief, mortifying fear that his fangs were about to pop out without permission.

Blake pressed a kiss to the corner of his mouth. "Are you gonna let me take care of you?"

"H-How?" Cass asked, trying to focus on words when every bit of blood was rushing south.

"I could stroke you again, if you wanted," Blake offered, apparently completely unaware he was dangerously close to giving Cass an aneurysm. "You seemed to like that, all hot and eager on my lap, squirming your ass against my dick like it was your first time jerking off. Or I could use my mouth on you. I've never done it before though. You'd have to tell me what feels good. Help me out, yeah?"

The thought of it—of Blake on his knees, swallowing Cass's cock, waiting for Cass to tell him he was *good*—almost made the point moot, as it had Cass a breath away from coming in his goddamn pants.

Blake seemed oblivious of the impending danger, mouthing along Cass's jaw, pressing hot kisses to his neck. "What do you think, hm? What sounds good?"

"What if—" Cass tried to find his breath, to find the words. "What if I wanted...more?"

Blake's lips paused on his throat, and then he was leaning back to peer down at Cass, what looked an awful lot like a smirk threatening to form. "You still trying to lose your *V* card this weekend, baby?"

Cass tried not to squirm, even as he felt his cheeks heat. "Would that be—would that be bad?"

His answer was Blake picking him up with two strong arms under Cass's ass—hello, secret masturbation fantasy number one—and then plopping him on the neatly made hotel bed, blanketing him with his body a second later.

Cass lifted his head for a kiss and was rewarded with Blake's mouth on his, tongue parting his lips with outrageous confidence. They made out long enough for Cass's head to go pleasantly fuzzy, his entire being focused on the feel of being kissed by Blake.

When he finally let Blake up for air—and Cass was panting too, whether from actual need or old reflex, he couldn't be sure—he realized they were both already somehow shirtless.

His eyes widened, taking Blake in. He had *such* a fucking nice body. Cass had always known, of course, but he hadn't had blanket permission to ogle before. He took advantage of it now, drinking in his fill, stroking his palms along Blake's broad shoulders, his muscled arms. "I can't believe I get to touch this."

Blake pressed a surprisingly chaste kiss to his lips. "Touch all you like."

"And you—we're gonna...?" Cass looked pleadingly at him, hoping he didn't have to finish his own sentence.

A familiar teasing glint lit up Blake's green eyes. "Oh, I don't know. Because see, I've kind of poured my heart out a bit, and all you've told me is that you're horny for my body."

"It's a *really* nice body though."

Blake slid down enough that his head was level with Cass's chest, his hands doing their own exploration of Cass's bare skin. "So is this one."

"I'm not—"

"Hush, baby. You're so pretty. You're the prettiest thing I've ever seen. I could do amazing, unspeakable things to this body."

Cass was nodding with possibly the greatest enthusiasm of his life. "Yes. Do those. Unspeakable things. Let's."

Blake tilted his head up to meet Cass's eyes, and he was still teasing, wasn't he? "But you never answered my question, did you, Cass? Do you like me?" He rubbed a thumb over Cass's nipple, smirking at Cass's gasp. "Huh, baby? Do you like me too? Tell me. Don't leave a guy hanging."

Cass narrowed his eyes. He had absolutely no doubt Blake knew—even if he hadn't figured it out before this trip—what a massive crush Cass had been harboring. "You're being a jerk, you know. You have no idea how long I've wanted to do this. You're so fucking *hot*. All the time. Walking around looking hot and acting sweet and...ugh!" He threw his hands up, covering his face.

His body started shaking shortly after, and he realized Blake was laughing, his face pressed against Cass's belly.

"Not funny," Cass muttered through his hands.

Blake lifted his head, smirking at him. "It would only be unfunny if I didn't feel the same way."

"You didn't though."

"I just didn't realize it," Blake said, nuzzling his head against Cass's stomach. "I'm not very smart."

Cass moved his hands from his face, frowning down at him. "You're plenty smart."

"Eh." Blake shrugged, popping up onto his knees. "Luckily you're smart enough for the both of us." He started wrestling with Cass's pants, unbuttoning them and pulling them off his legs. "And we're gonna need those smarts."

"Planning a naked study sesh, are you?"

Blake paused a moment, pants still in hand. "Something to think about," he said, seemingly to himself. And then to Cass, "We're gonna need those smarts because I have no fucking idea what I'm doing, and we want your first time to be good, don't we?"

Cass rose onto his elbows. "You can't just stick it in."

"I know *that* much." Blake rolled his eyes, as if he hadn't just told Cass he was completely clueless. "Did you pack lube, knowing you'd be trying to seduce creepy hotel dudes this vacation?"

"It's in my bag," Cass said, refusing to be embarrassed, no matter how hot his cheeks felt.

Blake just cocked a brow and hopped off the bed, returning with lube and condoms. Vampires couldn't give or get STIs, Danny had whispered to Cass as he was leaving, as some sort of last piece of vampire godfather sage wisdom. But Cass didn't have the courage to bring that up yet, not when Blake was looking kind of adorably determined, setting the lube and a seriously ambitious stack of condoms next to it.

"You get naked too," Cass ordered, poking at Blake's pants with his foot.

"Is that part of the process?" But Blake obliged, removing his joggers and underwear and flinging them onto the floor, to meet all their other clothes.

But God, he had a nice cock. It figured he'd be blessed in every way. Cass couldn't even be bitter about it anymore though. Not when Blake was *his* now.

That new presence in him rumbled happily. It liked that thought.

Blake peered down at Cass's naked form doubtfully, his hard cock bobbing at his stomach. "So I need to prep you, right? Should I turn you on your belly?"

Cass bit at his lip, holding back a smile. It was kind of cute that, even as the virgin, he was the one with more knowledge of how to go about banging each other's brains out. "No, we can do it like this. Or *I* could just—"

Blake lifted the small bottle of lube up high, as if Cass was going to snatch it out of his hands. "No, *I'm* gonna do it. I'm taking care of you, remember?"

Cass was ready to protest, but Blake's cock jerked along with his words, and Cass had a little moment of realization: Blake liked taking care of Cass. Like, the *horny* kind of liked it.

Blake settled down on his belly, in between Cass's legs. He was so *close* to all Cass's bits. Would it be a turn-off? He had just come to terms with being attracted to dudes at all; did he really want a dick in his face?

But when Cass peered down, Blake looked happy as he'd ever seen him, rubbing his cheeks against the inside of Cass's thigh like a damned cat, his stubble sending tickles up Cass's spine. "So smooth, baby."

Cass had never had much hair. Not on his chest or anywhere else. Well, there were *some* places; he just kept it neatly trimmed. But Blake didn't seem to mind.

He was still rubbing his head against Cass's skin when Cass felt the first lubed fingertip press against his hole. "*Oh—*"

He considered again letting Blake know about the "no just jamming things in" rule, but Blake was already shushing him. "Sh, baby. 'M not gonna hurt you."

And he didn't. He just rubbed that fingertip along Cass's most sensitive skin, seemingly in no hurry. Meanwhile, he started pressing kisses along Cass's stomach, his hips, every now and then brushing his lips along Cass's dick in a horrible tease.

It went long enough that Cass started squirming, just like he had on Blake's lap that morning. And maybe that had been the goal, because Blake was looking up at him, practically beaming.

"*Blake*," Cass whined.

"Yes, baby?"

"It doesn't have to be *this* slow."

"It doesn't?" Blake asked, all false innocence.

"I'll bite you," Cass threatened.

Blake didn't look at all frightened by the threat, but he did start pressing his fingertip in. And *oh*, that was nice. Really nice. His finger was so much bigger than Cass's own. Which led to a moment of panic: just his finger was that much bigger; what about his fucking dick?

But Blake still didn't seem to be in any hurry. He kept pressing his finger in, moving it about, eventually finding a spot that made Cass yelp and then stroking it mercilessly.

When Cass stared down at him, he just smirked. "Straight guys have prostates too."

He made Cass beg for the second finger and the third, content to press kisses along every inch of reachable skin, murmuring "take care of you" and "so pretty" over and over while Cass trembled beneath him.

Cass began to worry maybe Blake was delaying, that he wasn't aching to fuck Cass the way Cass was aching to be fucked. Eventually he found the strength to lift his head to ask, "Blake?"

Blake took one look at his concerned face and laughed before sitting up and showing Cass what his other hand had been up to: mainly holding his cock in a viselike grip, presumably to stop him from coming too soon. He was still rock-hard, little pearly drops of precum forming at the angry red tip.

Cass beamed in relief. "Oh, thank God."

"Did you think I didn't want this, baby? With you looking so pretty and trembling so nicely for me?"

That was all well and good, but he was still taking his sweet time. "I'm ready, okay?" Cass reassured. "So ready. You've taken really good care of me, I promise. And now you have to fuck me, or I'm going to lose my mind." Cass spread his legs wide, feeling foolish but hoping it would be some sort of appealing.

And apparently it was, because Blake did one hard swallow, and then he was tearing the condom wrapper off with almost supernatural speed, lubing himself up with much less delicacy then he'd been showing Cass's tender parts.

He pressed Cass's legs back, lining himself up. Cass found himself watching Blake's face as Blake watched himself entering him. He looked mesmerized, his plush mouth slack and his eyes heavy-lidded.

And then Blake pushed in deeper, and Cass couldn't watch anymore. He threw his head back, trying to breathe through the insane *fullness*. This was it. It was happening. Blake was *inside* him. Blake was taking his virginity. Blake was—

Blake was not moving. Blake was in fact holding incredibly still, looking at Cass almost fearfully.

"I'm not gonna break. You can move." Cass wrapped his legs around Blake's hips, pushing him deeper, and wound his arms around Blake's neck, pulling him closer. "Fuck me like you mean it, roomie."

He was rewarded with a desperate sound, one he'd never heard Blake make before, and then he was moving, a steady rhythm that reminded Cass of just how much more experience Blake had with this. But it was hard to be put out about it when he was using that experience to rock Cass's world.

Especially when Blake found *that* spot again, and when Cass made an especially pathetic sound, electricity shooting up his spine, Blake mercilessly found it again and again. Cass would have been embarrassed maybe, of the noises coming out of his mouth, if Blake wasn't also mindlessly chanting, "So good. So fucking good. So *good*."

Cass lost track of time, his mind going hazy with pleasure, and eventually Blake's moans took on a desperate turn. "I'm sorry, baby, I'm gonna come. You're too good. You're too fucking good."

And Cass would have been right there too, if he felt like stroking his own cock for even a second. But he didn't want to unwind his arms from Blake's neck, didn't want to be even an inch farther apart than they were now. If anything, he wanted him closer. So he pulled Blake down fully on top of him, Blake's arms coming up under his shoulders to find new purchase. "Yes, come. I've got you."

And Blake did, thrusting mercilessly until his hips stuttered to a finish, his breath hot against Cass's neck.

And before Cass could come down from the high of having made Blake—*his* Blake—come, Blake was moving down his body, swallowing Cass's cock like some sort of pro, and that was it, that was the end, Cass was coming in a fucking second. It would have maybe been mortifying if he hadn't just been dicked down so good.

They lay panting and sweating, bodies entwined together once again. Blake was looking down at him, a sort of secretive smile on his face.

"What?" Cass asked, his finger tracing the curve of Blake's lips.

"Your fangs are out," Blake said softly.

Cass's hand flew to his mouth. "Oh! Oh. I'm not hungry, I promise. I just—"

Blake grabbed his hand, lowering it, and pressed a kiss to his lips. "Don't worry, baby. If I had fangs, they'd have popped out too. That was fucking *awesome*."

Cass giggled, suddenly so giddy he thought he could float off the bed, fangs and all. "Yeah, it was pretty awesome." He snuggled into Blake's broad shoulder. "You don't mind? The face?"

"What did I tell you before? You're the prettiest thing I've ever seen."

Cass sighed happily. "We're gonna be good boyfriends, aren't we?"

Blake kissed his forehead. "We're gonna be the best."

"Even though I'm a vampire?"

"What have I always said?" Blake asked.

"Gym before class, that's how you gain mass," Cass recited dutifully. Blake even had it written on his whiteboard.

"Not what I meant," Blake scolded, stroking a hand down Cass's spine. "I've got your back. Always."

Seven

Epilogue

Blake

B lake woke slowly, blinking against the morning light streaming through their apartment's curtains. He clutched the warm bundle in his arms tighter, fingers dancing along the smooth skin of Cass's stomach, no pajamas on either of them to get in the way.

"Tickles," Cass murmured, clearly still half-asleep himself. He generally stayed up many hours later than Blake, his vampire body not needing as much sleep, but he loved to climb into bed in the last few hours and claim what he *did* need so they could both wake up together.

It suited Blake well—he'd grown used to falling asleep to the soft sounds of Cass typing on his laptop, or the quiet turn of pages when he was reading. And he liked that Cass was still as slow to wake as ever, despite his many other vampire changes.

"Happy graduation day," Blake whispered.

They'd be in different ceremonies, unfortunately—Cass with his biology department and Blake with the business school. But then there would be dinner with Blake's family and Cass's grandfather to celebrate.

Speaking of food—

"You should eat before we go, hm?" Blake asked, pressing a kiss to the back of Cass's neck.

Cass had kept feeding on Blake, although he couldn't—or wouldn't—do it weekly, afraid to take too much. Every other week, he went hunting, and Blake would go with him, staying close by in case Cass ran into any trouble.

Watching his back.

"Mm," Cass mumbled sleepily, turning to face him, his hair rumpled from sleep. "Hello."

Blake grinned at him. "Hi, baby. How do you want me?"

That seemed to wake Cass up fully, a glint forming in his blue eyes that Blake had come to think of as his inner vampire peeping out. Cass rose on an elbow, using his other arm to push Blake onto his back. "Just like this, I think."

He climbed up to straddle Blake's hips, his pert, naked ass settling on top of Blake's morning wood. Cass smiled almost shyly as he felt it. "You want to...?"

"Yeah," Blake said eagerly, reaching into the bedside table for lube.

Being fed on by Cass was always hot no matter what—the spike of pleasure from the bite, the intimacy of giving him exactly what he needed—but it was even better when they fucked at the same time. Which Blake supposed they did more often than not.

Blake got to work opening Cass up while Cass nosed along his neck, humming happily as he breathed Blake in. Ever since he'd turned, it was like he was addicted to Blake's scent, often rubbing his whole face into Blake's chest or the crook of Blake's shoulder when he wanted to calm himself down.

It didn't take long before Cass was ready for him, still relatively soft and open from their marathon session the night before.

"What first, baby?" Blake asked.

Cass shook his head, his nose brushing against Blake's shoulder. "All at once."

Of course. Blake's perfect, greedy boyfriend.

Cass wasted no time, biting into the crook of Blake's neck with his fangs as he lowered himself onto Blake's cock, growling in that adorable way he sometimes did when a feed was especially satisfying. Blake let the pleasure wash over him, rocking his hips lazily, listening to the sounds of Cass drinking from him, his perfect baby vampire, his favorite person in the world.

He'd thought he'd known the joys of living with Cass already, but nothing before could have compared to the past year and a half together: stealing kisses throughout the day, wrapping around each other every night, taking pleasure in each other's bodies countless times.

And this—this lazy, contented morning sex, all soft grunts and groans, Cass grinding on top of him, licking the bite closed as Blake stroked him without hurry.

They both finished on a sigh, and Cass lowered himself to cover Blake completely, or as completely as his small frame was capable.

Blake pressed a kiss to the side of his head. "You want to shower first, baby?"

"Mmph," Cass answered, which was probably as close to a yes as Blake was going to get from his sexed-out vampire.

Cass eventually stumbled out of the bed, and as soon as he heard the sounds of the shower running, Blake hopped out, hurrying to set up. He dug his gift out from the back of his nightstand, setting it on the kitchen table next to the flowers he'd hidden in the cabinet the day before.

He stole a kiss from a flushed, damp Cass on the way to his own shower, one he couldn't help but rush his way through. He tossed his clothes on as quickly as he could, and when he came out of the bedroom, there was Cass, holding the empty gift box in one hand, a ring in the other.

Blake wasn't any sort of jewelry connoisseur, but he was pretty sure he'd chosen well, especially seeing it in Cass's hands. It was a plain silver, with etchings of leaves around it. It would suit him. Masculine but...pretty.

"What's this?" Cass asked, his voice breathy.

"A promise. That I'm ready." Blake stepped closer, enfolding Cass's hands in his own. "You're not just my roommate or my boyfriend. You're the love of my life, and I'm not growing old without you. I want you to turn me this summer, after we move to Phoenix."

Cass looked stunned, his eyes searching Blake's face. "But...your family?"

"We'll tell them eventually, when we have to. There's no vampire law of secrecy, right? They'll understand. You're my person. My *mate*."

"Mate," Cass repeated, and there was a lower rumble in his voice, the one he sometimes got when his face changed.

"What do you say, baby?" Blake slid the ring onto Cass's finger. "Make me yours?"

The stunned expression left Cass's face, and then he was smiling at Blake like he'd never seen, his cheeks flushed with happiness. "Yes! And I'll help you with the transition. I'll take such good care of you."

Blake pressed his forehead to Cass's. "You've got my back, huh?"

"Always," Cass whispered.

Blake believed him. What else were roomies for?

The End.

About the Author

Grae Bryan has been reading romance since she was far too young to know any better. Her love for love stories spans all genres, and while her current series is of the paranormal variety, she knows she'll be exploring other worlds further down the line.

She lives in Arizona with her husband, who graciously shares space with all the imaginary men in her head. When not writing, she can generally be found reading more than is healthy, walking her monster-dog, or cuddling her demon-cat. She loves anything and everything gothic, strange, lovely, or cozy.

Find her online: graebryan.com
Join her Facebook reader group: Grae Bryan's Reader Den
Facebook: @GraeBryanAuthor
Instagram: @authorgraebryan
Sign up for her newsletter: graebryan.com/contact

www.ingramcontent.com/pod-product-compliance
Lightning Source LLC
Chambersburg PA
CBHW020810130626
46554CB00006B/2361